To all teachers, librarians and educators who
patiently and creatively grow our children every day.
Thank You!!

-Molly Covington

~~~~~~~~~~~~~~~~~

To all children enjoying the amazing sights, sounds,
souvenirs, trinkets and food at the
Albuquerque International Balloon Fiesta.

-Annette Puccini Crabtree

Bake-A-Cakey Books

Bake-A-Cakey Books LLC
www.bakeacakeybooks.com

Book design and production by Lois Bradley • www.loisbradley.com

The Albuquerque International

Balloon Fiesta® ABC Book

By

Molly Covington

Illustrated by

Annette Puccini Crabtree

A is for Albuquerque.

B is for Balloon

C

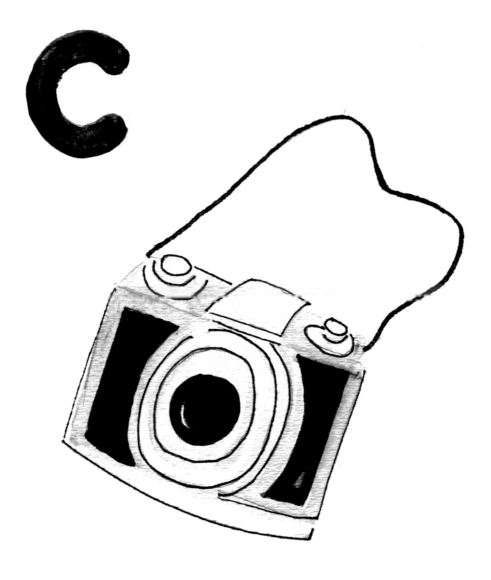

C is for Camera with lots of spare room.

D

D is for Donuts.

E is for Envelope.

F is for Fiesta, meaning "party" so don't mope.

G is for Gondola.

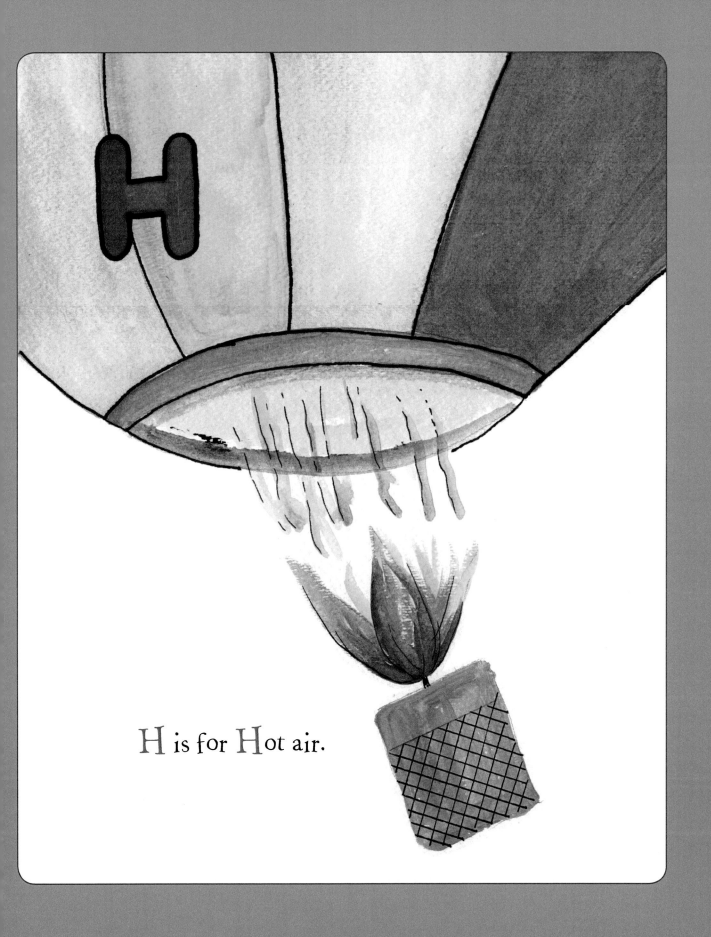

H is for Hot air.

I is for International people from everywhere.

J is for Java.

K is for Kiosk, so many to choose from you might just get lost.

L is for Light from the flames glowing bright.

M is for Magical.

N is for Night.

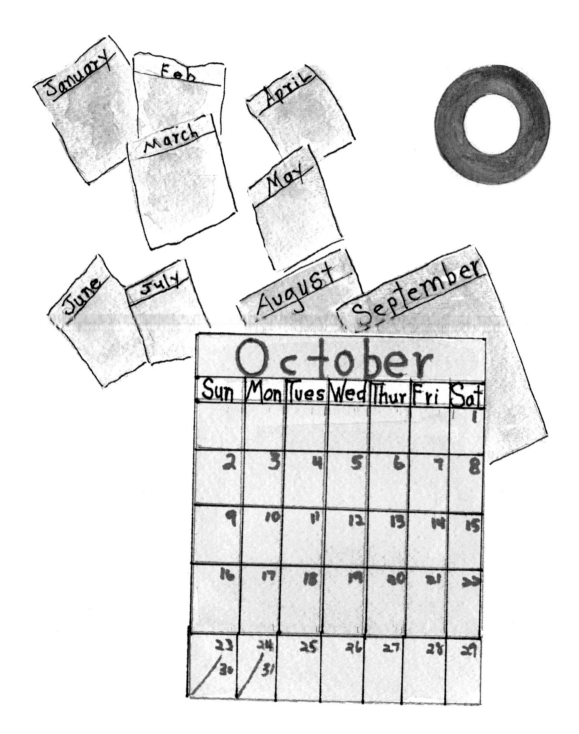

O is for October.

P is for Pilot or Pin.

Q is for Qualifying in games to win.

R is for Rainbow.

S is for Sky.

T is for Trinkets and goodies to buy.

U is for Ultimate fireworks show.

V is for Vacation, the best that I know.

W is for Weather, I hope that it rocks!

Then maybe we'll witness the Albuquerque boX.

Y

Y is for Yawn, 'cuz it's early, you see. But it's totally worth it which brings us to Z.

Z is for
Zebras.
How awesome
they look!

And that

is the

END

of our

ABC Book.

Made in the USA
San Bernardino, CA
26 December 2018